UH-OH, DODO!

By Jennifer Sattler

BOYDS MILLS PRESS
AN IMPRINT OF HIGHLIGHTS
Honesdale, Pennsylvania

Boyds Mills Press, Inc.
815 Church Street
Honesdale, Pennsylvania 18431
boydsmillspress.com
Printed in China

ISBN: 978-1-59078-929-2
Library of Congress Control Number: 2012947460
First edition
The text of this book is set in CCDoohickery and Montara Gothic.
The illustrations are done in acrylic and colored pencil.

10 9 8 7 6 5 4 3 2 1

To Mayzie and Lilia
and the memory of trying to get you from point A to point B . . .
the fun way
—JS

This is Dodo.

Dodo loves
to walk
with his Mama.

Today they are going someplace really special.

Dodo's feet are ready for adventure!

He can't believe

his toes are so

talented!

When he walks,
Dodo likes to sing loudly
for everyone to enjoy!

Dodo sees some
funny-shaped rocks.
This gets him thinking,
"Why not start
a funny-shaped
rock collection?"

Dodo is very good at making friends.

Sometimes
Dodo holds onto
a leg that isn't
his Mama's
by mistake.

. . . but Mama is always close by.

"Now, Dodo," says Mama,
"when we get to the top,
no peeking!"

After an exciting day,
it's time for the long walk home.

UHHH-OHHH, DODO!